LULU'S
Mysterious Mission

JUDITH VIORST

illustrated by KEVIN CORNELL
jacket by LANE SMITH

SCHOLASTIC INC.

ISBN 978-0-545-86091-8

Text copyright © 2014 by Judith Viorst. Illustrations copyright © 2014 by Kevin Cornell.
All rights reserved. Published by Scholastic Inc., 557 Broadway, New York, NY 10012, by arrangement with Atheneum Books for Young Readers, an imprint of Simon & Schuster Children's Publishing Division. SCHOLASTIC and associated logos are trademarks and/or registered trademarks of Scholastic Inc.

12 11 10 9 8 7 6 5 4 3 2 1   15 16 17 18 19 20/0

Printed in the U.S.A.   40

First Scholastic printing, March 2015

The text for this book is set in Officina Sans.
The illustrations for this book are rendered in graphite and watercolor on paper and then digitally manipulated.

To the Viorst grandsons:
Nathaniel, Benjamin, Isaac, Toby, and Bryce
—J. V.

For Kim, who holds my hand
—K. C.

STOP! *Don't begin the*

I need to tell you. And I think I'd better

This isn't a book about Lulu's Mysterious Mission. It's actually about Lulu's Babysitter. And that's what I wanted to call it except two kids that I know, Benjamin and Nathaniel, kept telling me that *Lulu's Babysitter* was a really boring title. Which means that the name of this book has absolutely nothing at all to do with the story I'm writing.

YOU HAVE NOW BEEN WARNED!

Wait! Now that I have warned you, I am feeling a tiny bit guilty.

first chapter just yet. There's something

tell it to you right now.

Like maybe it isn't fair to trick
readers like that. Like maybe
there ought to be a law that what's
INSIDE a book has to somehow
match up with the NAME of the
book. So maybe—I'm not *promising*,
but just maybe—I'll put in some
stuff about a Mysterious Mission.

Meanwhile, either return this
book or keep reading. You'll find
out what happens when Lulu
meets up with Ms. Sonia Sofia
Solinsky, who is definitely not your
Mary Poppins–type babysitter.

And you *might* find out about a
Mysterious Mission.

chapter one

But first let's go find Lulu, who is in the living room screeching "No! No! No!" although she doesn't screech much anymore. However, the news she was hearing from her mom and her dad was so utterly, totally SHOCKING that it not only started her screeching but almost shocked her into throwing one of her heel-kicking, arm-waving, on-the-floor tantrums. Lulu, however, thinks of herself

as too grown-up now to throw tantrums. Which also means she thinks of herself as grown-up enough to go with her mom and her dad on the trip they just told her that they would be taking WITHOUT HER.

When Lulu had finished screeching, she fiercely glared at her mom and her dad and asked them—in a not-too-nice voice— these questions:

"How can you have a good time if I'm not there?"

And "Who's going to take care of me, and how can you be positive that this person won't kidnap me and hold me for ransom?"

And "Or maybe she'll stop feeding me and start yelling at me and hitting me and locking me down in the basement with the rats." (Okay, that isn't technically a question.)

When Lulu was done, her mom and her dad looked at each other, then answered—very carefully. For even though their daughter wasn't the serious pain in the butt that she used to be, she wasn't the easiest girl in the world to be parents to when she didn't get her way.

"First of all," said Lulu's dad, "there are no rats in our basement. As a matter of fact, we don't even HAVE a basement."

"But even if we did," said Lulu's mom, "we'd never hire a sitter who'd lock you up in it. Or starve you or hit you or yell at you or kidnap you."

"Or," added Lulu's dad, "hold you for ransom."

"And if you were held for ransom," Lulu's mom assured Lulu, patting her oh-so-lovingly on the cheek, "we'd pay whatever it took to get you back."

"But," Lulu pointed out, removing her mom's patting hand from her cheek, "if instead of paying the ransom, you'd let me come with you, this trip of yours would cost a lot less money."

Lulu's dad explained that as much as they loved and adored their precious only child, they wanted to have—for the first time since they'd been parents—a private grown-ups-only vacation together. And that even though they wouldn't be having the kind of fun they had with their fabulous Lulu, they would be having a DIFFERENT kind of fun.

"You mean BETTER fun," grumped Lulu. "You'll have better fun without me. And you won't even care when I get sick and die."

chapter two

Lulu's mom started crying at the thought of poor little Lulu, left behind and dead of a broken heart. "Maybe . . . ," she sniffled to Lulu's dad, "maybe we ought to stay home. Or take her with us. Maybe we are being too unkind."

It's at this point in every argument that Lulu almost always gets her way because her mom and her dad just cannot BEAR it when their darling is displeased. It's right at this point that Lulu almost always gets what she wants because her mom and her dad give up and give in. Except on those rare occasions—like now, for instance—when they try NOT to.

Lulu's dad cleared his throat, and in a strong, firm voice replied to Lulu's mom. "No," he said. "We're going. She's staying. THAT'S what we decided and"—he took a deep breath—"we're sticking to it."

He then turned to Lulu and said, "But you don't have a thing to worry about, dearest darling. Because, after much research, we've hired the best babysitter in town—maybe the world—to take care of you the week that we're away."

"Babysitter?" Lulu gasped. "Babysitter? Babysitters sit babies, and I'm no baby."

(Lulu thinks she's no baby because she plays a tough game of Scrabble, goes by herself to the corner store to buy milk, gets good reports from her teachers, earns some money walking dogs, rides a bike with no hands, and has pierced ears. She's also on the softball team, the swim team, and the debate team; has recently started learning the trombone; and is going to be a crossing guard next year. And what Lulu wants to know is why a person who can do all that would need a person called a *baby*sitter.)

"Call her what you want, but her name," Lulu's mom said soothingly, "is Ms. Sonia Sofia Solinsky, a trained professional. And we're sure, dear, that if you, dear, will give her, dear, a chance, dear, the two of you will get along just fine."

"In fact," said Lulu's dad, "she's moving in this afternoon. We'll show her around the house, and maybe you two can start to bond before your mom and I leave tomorrow morning."

(Tomorrow morning? They're leaving tomorrow morning? How come Lulu is only now being told that her mom and her dad are leaving tomorrow morning?

How come she wasn't told earlier? How come she wasn't given time to prepare? As the person who's writing this story, I take full responsibility for this decision. Because anyone who knows Lulu like I know Lulu wouldn't want to give her time to prepare.)

"I'm going up to my room," said Lulu to her mom and her dad. "And maybe I'll come down and maybe I won't. But while I'm up there," she added as she loudly tromped up the stairs, "I'm planning to be very very unhappy."

chapter three

Up in her room, along with being very very unhappy, Lulu was trying to figure out what to do. Actually, she knew WHAT to do: get rid of the babysitter so her mom and her dad would have no one to leave her with. All she needed to figure out was HOW.

She went to her computer—yes, she has her own computer; she has her own *everything*—and typed in "How To Get Rid of a Babysitter." But nothing too helpful came up, so Lulu started making a list of possibilities, and as she wrote she chanted this little chant:

Eeny meeny miney mo,
That babysitter's got to go.

While Lulu was chanting and making her list, the doorbell rang and a voice boomed through the house, a voice that sounded to Lulu like real bad news. "Sonia Sofia Solinsky," it said. "At your service."

Lulu heard the gentle murmurs of her mom and her dad, interspersed with Ms. Solinsky's boom, and the quiet patter of their feet, interspersed with Ms. Solinsky's clomp, and then someone (either her mom or her dad) was knocking softly at her bedroom door, with Ms. Solinsky bellowing, "The eagle has landed, Lulu. Open up."

("The eagle has landed"? That's how Ms. Solinsky says hello?)

Lulu, thinking fast, took off her shoes, jumped into bed, and huddled pitifully underneath her comforter, hoping to make all three of them believe that she had suddenly been struck down with some

dreadful disease. And so, when she heard her mom calling, "Come out, my darling, and meet Ms. Solinsky," she said, "I think that I just got real sick."

"Probably not," said Lulu's dad. "You looked perfectly fine to me only an hour ago."

"But I'm not fine now," Lulu replied. "I think I'm very sick. And, anyway, I'm definitely contagious."

"Not a problem," Ms. Solinsky boomingly replied. "I never catch anything."

She then—the nerve!—turned the doorknob, opened Lulu's bedroom door, and marched herself straight over to Lulu's bed.

chapter four

The sight of Ms. Solinsky, with her long unsmiling face and her hair yanked back in a tight little, mean little bun, was not the kind to gladden a young girl's heart. She was dressed in some sort of uniform that a General of All Generals might wear, with binoculars and a metal

canteen hanging down from the belt
that held up her pants, and a jacket
bedecked with several silver medals,
along with rows of badges and ribbons
and stars. On her feet were heavy,
thick-soled, high-top, lace-up combat
boots, the kind that could stomp
almost anything into dust. And over her
shoulder she hauled a bulging duffel
bag, stuffed from bottom to top with
who knows what. Anyone else, after
taking one look at Sonia Sofia Solinsky,
would have shivered and shuddered and
instantly said, "I surrender."

(Maybe you're starting to wonder why Lulu's mom and Lulu's dad would ever hire someone who would wear a menacing uniform and combat boots. All I can tell you is, first, everyone said that Ms. Solinsky was the best babysitter in town—maybe the world—and, second, she may not have looked like that when they interviewed her.)

But she sure looked like that now, and, as I already pointed out, anyone else would have shivered and said, "I surrender."

Not Lulu.

Indeed, when Ms. Solinsky reached her hand out for a handshake, Lulu, instead of politely reaching back, crossed her arms across her chest and tucked her hands

emphatically into her armpits. "Maybe you can't catch something from me, but I," said Lulu, "might catch something from you. And maybe what I might catch could make me even sicker than I already am."

"Well, aren't you the sensible one!" Ms. Solinsky exclaimed. "But still—no problem." She dug into her duffel bag, pulled out a packet of disinfectant wipes, and briskly wiped down her hands—first left, then right. "I've just killed off my germs, which means you can't catch

something from me," she said to Lulu. "So now"—she reached out again—"shall we shake hands?"

Although there was a question mark at the end of this last sentence, this wasn't a question.

Lulu shook hands.

After the handshake Ms. Solinsky told Lulu's mom and her dad that if they wanted to pack for their trip, she would stay with Lulu and keep her company. "We'll do just fine," she assured them as they gratefully rushed from the room, moving so fast that they didn't see Lulu frantically shaking her head and mouthing (so Ms. Solinsky wouldn't hear her), "Don't go."

The minute they were gone Ms. Solinsky brought her unsmiling face down close to Lulu's and said, "That I'm-so-sick routine may work out great in a storybook or in a movie, but don't waste my time trying it on me. You're in excellent health, and I want you on your feet, in your shoes, standing tall, arms straight down at your sides in exactly"—she looked at her wristwatch—"ninety seconds."

No grown-up in Lulu's entire life had ever dared to talk to her that way. And no grown-up, Lulu decided, would be allowed to. And so, without saying a word, she pulled the comforter over her head and pressed her body hard into the mattress. She could hear Ms. Solinsky counting down—"eighty seconds . . . sixty seconds . . . thirty-five . . . twenty-five . . . fifteen seconds . . . time's up." And then, without taking a breath, Ms. Solinsky swooped an astonished Lulu out of her bed, set her onto her feet and into her shoes, pushed back her shoulders, lifted her chin, and pressed a firm palm against her droopy spine.

And—what do you know!—there was Lulu, standing tall, head high, her arms straight down at her sides. Looking good. But not quite good enough.

"Hmm," muttered Ms. Solinsky as she walked around her, carefully checking her out, "I see we have a lot of work to do."

chapter five

From that time on, until Lulu's mom and her dad went away the next morning, Lulu had not one moment just with them. Whenever they knocked at the bedroom door, Ms. Solinsky bellowed, "We're still bonding," though, in fact, what they mostly were doing was glaring. At dinner Ms. Solinsky was right at Lulu's side. And early on Saturday morning, when Lulu's mom and her dad were kissing her good-bye and Lulu was getting ready to make-believe faint in one last effort to stop them from going, Ms. Solinsky was stationed directly behind her, holding tight to the back of her skirt so she couldn't fall.

As her mom and her dad headed out to the taxi, Lulu heard her mom saying, "If things don't work out with Lulu . . ."

And her dad saying, ". . . and it's just possible that they won't . . ."

And her mom saying, ". . . call us, and we'll take the next plane home."

To which Ms. Solinsky firmly replied, "When I'm the babysitter, things ALWAYS work out."

"We'll see about that," Lulu said to herself, preparing for Plan B, which was doing whatever she had to do to get her parents to take the next plane home.

Then the door slammed, and Lulu was all alone with Ms. Solinsky, trained professional.

chapter six

$\mathcal{M}\!s.$ Solinsky smiled at Lulu with the kind of smile that an alligator might give you just before that alligator ate you for dinner. It was not the kind of smile that made the person being smiled at want to smile back. It was more the kind of smile that gave you a headache, a stomachache, and a lump in your throat.

"Maybe I really AM sick," Lulu told her.

"Could be," said Ms. Solinsky. "But lucky for you, I've got just the cure. A nice brisk run around the block—three times. It will put some fresh air into your lungs and some pink into your cheeks.

And it will give you a great appetite for the bean-and-beet omelet I'm making for your breakfast."

(Lulu—you won't be surprised to hear—doesn't do brisk runs or bean-and-beet omelets. The last time she had a brisk run was when she was briskly running away from Mr. B, a delightful brontosaurus who, after a little misunderstanding, became her best friend. And a bean-and-beet omelet sounded like something her dog-walking-partner and sort-of-friend Fleischman would eat because, although utterly disgusting, it was so good for him.)

Now those of us who know Lulu would have expected her to screech, "Brisk run? Bean-and-beet omelet? You must be kidding me!" But screeching wasn't part of Lulu's Plan B. Instead, she said, in a fake sweet voice, "I'll just go upstairs, Ms. Solinsky, and get my sneakers."

"And be quick about it," answered Ms. Solinsky.

"Yes, sir," said Lulu, clicking her heels and saluting at the same time.

"I am not amused," said Ms. Solinsky.

As Lulu headed up the stairs, she cheerfully, though softly, chanted this chant:

Eeny meeny miney mo,
That babysitter's got to go.
Hot or cold or sun or snow,
That babysitter's got to go.

chapter seven

When Lulu reached the second floor she didn't go to her bedroom to get her sneakers. That hadn't ever been a part of her plan. Instead, she went to the bathroom, opened the window, and climbed out onto the tree that grew there. A tree she had very often climbed onto and down from—right down into her backyard.

Her plan, when she reached the ground, was to find a hiding place in the neighborhood while Ms. Solinsky waited for her inside, waited and waited until she finally went upstairs and found that open window. After which Lulu intended to keep on hiding while Ms. Solinsky kept on searching for her. After which Lulu intended to still keep hiding while Ms. Solinsky—trained professional though she might very well be—would have to call Lulu's mom and her dad to say, "I've lost your daughter. You need to get on the next plane and come home."

As to what, exactly, they'd do to the babysitter who had lost their precious daughter, Lulu was quite certain that they would get rid of her, hopefully having first stripped her of every one of her medals and ribbons and badges and stars. As to what, exactly, Lulu planned to tell her mom and her dad about why she had hidden from the babysitter, Lulu was quite certain that between now and then she would figure something out.

"Eeny meeny miney mo," Lulu chanted again as she slid down the tree trunk. "That babysitter's got to go," she chanted as her two feet hit the ground. "Hot or cold or sun or snow," she continued, pulling her socks up and tucking her shirt in. But before she could finish another "That babysitter's got to go," a loud "ahem!" disturbed her happy mood.

Standing at strict attention at the bottom of the tree—and what, in heaven's name, was she doing out there?—was none other than Ms. Sonia Sofia Solinsky.

"What, in heaven's name, are you doing out here?" Lulu fake-sweetly asked her. "I was just getting ready to meet you by the front door."

"I very much doubt that," said Ms. Solinsky, scowling down at Lulu and shaking a stern finger in her face. "But

I'm warning you, don't bother trying that climb-out-the-window-and-down-the-tree nonsense again. Believe me, I know tricks that you've never dreamed of. Besides which, you were already wearing your sneakers."

She then grabbed Lulu's hand and said, "It's time for our brisk run. And forget what you're thinking—I'm not letting go."

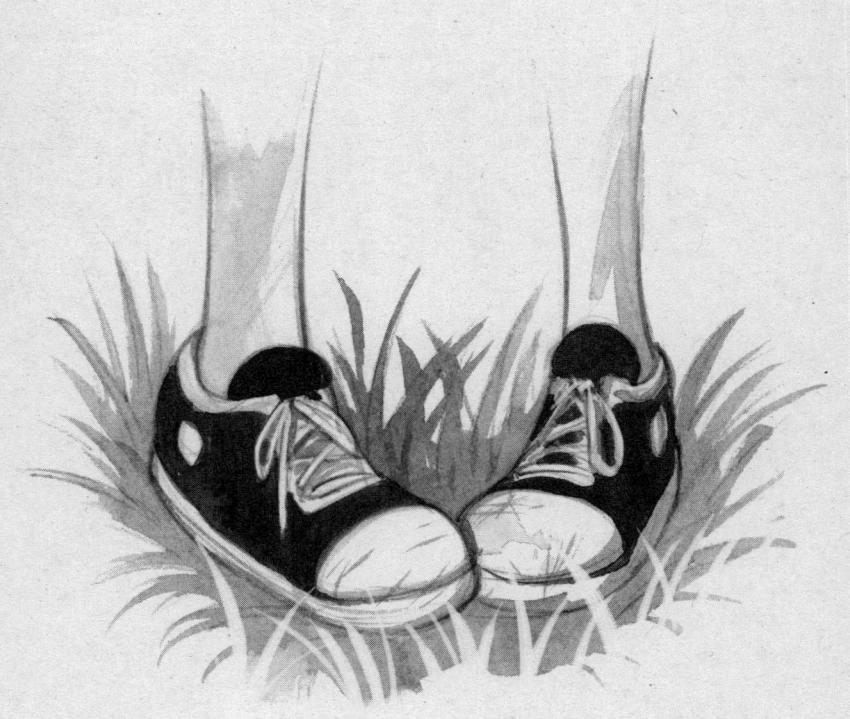

chapter eight

Three laps around the block later, Lulu was back in her own kitchen eating a hideous, horrible bean-and-beet omelet. She was also still plotting how to get rid of Ms. Sonia Sofia Solinsky, who wasn't sounding that easy to get rid of.

"It's almost time for my trombone

lesson," Lulu told Ms. Solinsky. "It's just a few blocks away. I can go by myself."

"You won't be going anywhere by yourself," said Ms. Solinsky. "I promised your folks I'd watch over you, and I will. And since this morning's escapade, I will be watching over you very carefully." She then explained what "very carefully" meant:

"It means that I will be going with you to your trombone lesson today and to the front door of your school to drop you off and pick you up every day next week, as well as to the bathroom every night when you take a bath, as well as to your dog-walking job on Monday, Tuesday, Wednesday, Thursday, and Friday. Any questions?"

"Yes, sir," said Lulu. "Will you also be going along with me when I throw up your delicious bean-and-beet omelet?"

"I am not amused," said Ms. Solinsky.

"Me either," Lulu said to her, heading out the door with her trombone and—of course!—Ms. Solinsky. And shortly thereafter the two of them were standing outside the house of—I'll explain this to you in a second—Harry Potter.

chapter nine

So let me explain.

Harry Potter, to everyone's bemusement and confusement, is Lulu's trombone teacher's actual name, which forces him to have to reply, whenever he meets someone new, "Sorry. No. *Not* Harry Potter, boy wizard. The *other* Harry Potter, trombone teacher." He also, much too often, has to put up with all kinds of incredibly stupid jokes about spells and potions and wands and flying broomsticks. It makes me kind of wonder, since I am the person writing this story, if maybe I should have found him a different name. But though I'm the first to admit that this might have saved him a lot of trouble, sometimes a writer has to make tough choices.

By this time, Harry Potter had opened
his door and invited Lulu and Ms. Solinsky
to come inside and have a seat in the
living room. "There's something I need
to take care of," he told them, "so make
yourselves at home. I'll be ready for you in
just a couple of minutes."

Ms. Solinsky—her posture perfect;
her mouth in a stern, straight line—sat
down at one end of Harry Potter's couch.

Lulu—chin on the palms of her hands, and elbows on her knees—sat far down on the other end of the couch. A clock ticked loudly in the unfriendly silence.

All of a sudden, Ms. Solinsky leaped up off the couch. She was coughing and sneezing and gasping and wheezing! And coughing and sneezing and gasping and wheezing! Then coughing and sneezing and gasping and wheezing some more!

"Cats! There must be cats in this house!"
she said in a croaky voice, rubbing her
now bright-pink and watery eyes. And
just as she spoke, Harry Potter returned,
saying apologetically, "Sorry to keep
you waiting, but I really had to feed my
hungry cats."

"To which," Ms. Solinsky announced,
dabbing a handkerchief to her eyes, "I'm
sorry to say I am seriously allergic."

"But," Lulu asked, displaying (I'm sorry to say) a most unfortunate absence of sympathy, "weren't you bragging just yesterday that—and I'm quoting directly—'I never catch *anything*?'"

"An allergy," Ms. Solinsky said in the iciest of voices, "is something that you *have*, not something you *catch*." She then explained that in order to keep her allergy from getting much, much worse, she would need to wait for Lulu outside the house.

"But RIGHT outside the house," she told Harry Potter. "Ready to take charge of her the instant that her trombone lesson is done."

"We'll see who's taking charge here," Lulu said—but just to herself. And then, but just to herself, she chanted:

Eeny meeny miney mo,
That babysitter's got to go.

Hot or cold or sun or snow,
That babysitter's

Soon, not later; fast, not slow,
That baby

got to go.

sitter's got to go.

And then, but just to herself, she
said, "And now I know what to do to
get her going!"

chapter ten

Lulu made a lot of mistakes during her trombone lesson because her brain was busy with her new plan. And as soon as her lesson was done and she was back upstairs in her room, she sent out messages by e-mail and cell phone.

All the messages said the same thing.

All of them were sent to Lulu's friend Mabel.

Do you remember Mabel? Of course you don't. Neither do I. But I am about to. And right now the most important thing that all of us need to remember about Mabel is that she is the owner of two cats. Because Mabel plus Two Cats equals Plan C.

Which is why each of Lulu's messages

was marked top secret and said: "Bring
your cats to my house right now for a
sleepover," though some of them said it
like this: "Top ckret—brng ur katz 2 my
hse rite now 4 a sleepovr."

  While Lulu waited for Mabel she chanted
her chant and, in between verses,
pondered three questions.

Eeny meeny miney mo,
That babysitter's got to go.

Q: How long would it take two cats that had been secretly stashed in Ms. Solinsky's bedroom to make her start coughing and sneezing and gasping and wheezing?

Hot or cold or sun or snow,
That babysitter's got to go.

Q: How long would it take for her allergy to go from serious to much, much worse?

Soon, not later; fast, not slow,
That babysitter's got to go.

Q: And how long before she had to telephone Lulu's mom and her dad to say, "Cats! I can't live with cats! Your daughter's attacking me with cats! You need to get on the next plane and come home"?

Up and down and to and fro,
That babysitter's got to go.

Less than ten minutes after Lulu had
sent out her urgent messages, she looked
out her bedroom window and there was
Mabel. She was pumping sturdily down
the street and balancing in the basket of
her bike something craftily covered up by
a blanket. That covered-up something,
Lulu was sure, was the carrier people use

when they take a pet on a plane or to a sleepover.

Mabel was a girl who could be counted on to understand "top secret."

Lulu rushed down the stairs and was heading out the front door to meet Mabel when she heard a voice roaring somewhere overhead, "Halt! Stop! Cease and desist! Don't move! Hold it right there!"

Lulu halted.

But then the voice continued, "Listen up, Mabel. This means you. Halt or you will be under arrest for trespassing."

Lulu ran outside and looked around for Ms. Solinsky, whose voice (as all of us know, of course) it was. But the sitter was nowhere in sight until another "Cease

and desist" made Lulu look upward. And
there, her combat boots firmly planted on
the roof of the house and her loud voice
made louder by a megaphone, was Sonia
Sofia Solinsky, her medals gleaming in the
afternoon sun.

And there, just beyond Lulu's driveway,
was the usually super-cool Mabel, off her
bike and stuttering, "But . . . but . . . but . . .
but . . ."

"Time to leave now," said Ms. Solinsky

to an astounded Mabel. "Trespassing is a criminal offense."

"Mabel isn't trespassing. I invited her. She's visiting me," said Lulu. "What is your problem?"

"No problem," said Ms. Solinsky, "because I know from your top secret messages that Mabel has been invited to come with her cats. And since I'm severely allergic to cats, she and they will have to leave. Immediately."

Mabel, cool girl though she was, was feeling alarmed at the possibility of maybe going to prison for criminal trespassing. "Sorry, Lulu!" she shouted, and then, accompanied by meowing sounds from her basket, she jumped on her bike and swiftly pedaled away.

When Ms. Solinsky came down from the roof, Lulu indignantly asked her, "How did you know that Mabel was bringing cats? How did you know what I wrote in my top secret messages? How did you ever find out what I was doing in the privacy of my own bedroom?"

"I have my ways," Ms. Solinsky replied. "I am a trained professional. Which is why I'm hired by parents all over town—maybe the world—to babysit their especially difficult children."

Lulu, more indignant than ever, glared at Ms. Solinsky. "Are you telling me that my mom and my dad think that I'm an especially difficult—"

"I'm not," Ms. Solinsky broke in, "telling you anything. I'm merely pointing out that, thanks to my training, I'm able to know when a person is not really sick, or is planning to climb out a window and go into hiding, or is writing top secret messages, which—thanks to my training—I'm able to read immediately."

Lulu moved on from indignant to outraged. "Isn't it rude," she demanded, "to read messages that haven't been sent to you?"

"Not as rude as bringing in cats when a person's allergic to cats," replied Ms. Solinsky.

After which the two of them had nothing whatsoever to say till Lulu's bedtime.

chapter eleven

You might imagine that Lulu, getting ready to go to bed, was feeling discouraged. Wrong! Lulu is not a girl who discourages easily, in spite of the fact that her sick plan, her hide plan, her bring-in-the cats-plan—all of them!—had failed. No, Lulu was not discouraged. She was . . . thinking.

She was thinking that she had just finished spending a whole, entire, totally bossed-around Saturday in the company of Sonia Sofia Solinsky. And THAT WAS ENOUGH. THAT WAS MORE THAN ENOUGH! She promised herself that by the end of Sunday, she was absolutely, positively, utterly, no doubt about it getting this babysitter out of her life.

Lulu lay in bed thinking, and chanting her chant:

Eeny meeny miney mo,
That babysitter's got to go.

Hot or cold or sun or snow,
That babysitter's got to go.

Soon, not later; fast, not slow,
That babysitter's got to go.

Up and down and to and fro,
That babysitter's got to go.

Forehead, belly, knee, and toe,
That babysitter's got to go.

Lulu tossed and turned in her bed—
thinking, chanting, thinking, chanting—
and then she smiled a wide and wicked
smile. She had another plan (and yes, I
know that it's her fourth plan, Plan D),
but this was the one she was certain
was going to work. For tomorrow
Lulu intended to teach Ms. Sonia
Sofia Solinsky the true meaning of an
especially difficult child.

chapter twelve

On Sunday morning Ms. Solinsky awakened Lulu early, telling her to get ready for another brisk run and another bean-and-beet omelet. Lulu leaped out of bed and rushed around the room to get ready, but NOT for another brisk run and horrid omelet.

The first thing she did—and this took enormous effort—was to push her dresser against her bedroom door, wedging it under the doorknob to make it hard, almost impossible, for Ms. Sonia Sofia Solinsky to come in.

Next she turned on her stereo and
television set, raising the volume as
loudly as it would go, and joining in,
just as loudly, with some truly terrible
tunes on her trombone. (Lulu wasn't
all that great at playing the trombone;
she made it sound like a hippo with a
stomachache—but I'd rather you didn't

tell her that I said so.) She finally, very carefully, put earplugs in her ears, and waited for the pounding at the door.

It didn't take long at all for Ms. Solinsky to be pounding at the door.

"Turn off that noise," she commanded, "and open up—now!"

But although she spoke and pounded so loudly that Lulu could hear her in spite of the noise and the earplugs, Lulu sweetly answered, "Sorry, can't hear you."

Ms. Solinsky kept pounding and pushing at Lulu's bedroom door, demanding, "Turn off that noise and open up!"

Lulu kept sweetly repeating, "Sorry, can't hear you."

Then Ms. Solinsky used both of her fists to pound against the door, yelling, "Turn off that noise and open up!"

Once again Lulu replied, "Sorry, can't hear you."

Then Ms. Solinsky raised one of her

feet (remember those heavy combat boots?) and aimed a mighty kick at Lulu's door, roaring as she kicked (and roaring's much louder than either commanding, demanding, or yelling), "TURN OFF THAT NOISE AND OPEN UP RIGHT NOW!"

And Lulu, just as sweetly as before, once again replied, "Sorry, can't hear you."

Next came a long and what some might call a terrifying pause. Then Ms. Solinsky bellowed (which is even louder than roaring), "DON'T YOU DARE SAY SORRY TO ME. I KNOW THAT YOU CAN HEAR

ME. SO NOW HEAR THIS: I AM
COMING IN!"

The next thing Lulu heard
was Ms. Solinsky running to
the end of the hall and then
running back—full speed—
toward her bedroom door.
And the next thing Lulu saw
was Ms. Solinsky crashing
through that heavy door and

knocking down the dresser blocking the door. Once past all these obstacles, she turned off Lulu's loud stereo and TV, after which she put her combat boots to use again by stomping Lulu's trombone into dust.

There were broken bits of door and dresser all over Lulu's bedroom. A lampshade was crushed; a chair was minus

one arm; the trombone was ruined, of course; and some green gooey glop, which used to be Lulu's science experiment, had dribbled out of its jar and now was stickily, stinkily splattered on the rug. Lulu studied the mess in her room and smiled a very big, very satisfied smile. Because, strange as it may seem to you, things were going exactly as she had planned.

chapter twelve
and
one half

As you've probably already noticed, we're more than halfway through this story, and I still haven't mentioned Lulu's Mysterious Mission. But before you start complaining, kindly keep in mind that I warned you that I might not. On the other hand, I also said that maybe—just maybe—I might, and I still might. So calm down.

chapter thirteen

As Lulu and Ms. Solinsky stared
at each other across the wreckage of
the room, Lulu began to chant her
little chant:

Eeny meeny
miney mo,
That babysitter's
got to go.

Hot or cold
or sun or snow,
That babysitter's
got to go.

Soon, not later; fast,
not slow,
That babysitter's
got to go.

Up and down
and to and fro,
That babysitter's
got to go.

Forehead, belly,
knee, and toe,
That babysitter's
got to go.

Ha-ha-ha
and ho-ho-ho,
That babysitter's
GOT TO GO.

This time, however, Lulu didn't bother
to chant her chant secretly—under
her breath, to herself, or alone in her
bed. Instead, she chanted it loudly and
outrageously
and shamelessly,
while standing
face to face with Ms. Solinsky.

Who was not amused.

"You are," she told Lulu, "an impudent,
insolent, insubordinate child! Impossible!
Incorrigible! Insufferable!"

"I'm not quite sure what all those words mean," said Lulu to Ms. Solinsky. "Why don't you give me a minute to look them up?"

"I am not amused," said Ms. Solinsky.

"But *you* are in trouble," said Lulu. "In really big trouble. I'm taking pictures"—and that's what (*click, click, click*) she started doing—"of how you completely and totally wrecked my room. And"—(*click, click, click*)—"I'm ready to send them, right this minute, to my mom and my dad."

"And why would you do that?" asked Ms. Solinsky.

"Because when they see what you've done to my room," said Lulu, "I'm sure they'll be flying back home on the very next plane."

(Well, what do you know?! Just as you maybe suspected! This was Lulu's Plan D, and it has worked!)

"I did what had to be done," Ms. Solinsky told Lulu. "I make no apologies. That's what it means to be a trained professional."

"But that's probably not what it means to be," Lulu said, "and I'm quoting directly, 'the best babysitter in town— maybe the world.'"

"Let me say once again that I make no apologies," Ms. Solinsky told Lulu. "But clearly my training to be a babysitter wasn't nearly as exhaustive or effective as my training to be a spy."

WHOA! WHOA! WHOA! WHOA! WHAT WAS *THAT*? *WHAT* IN THE WORLD WAS *THAT*? *WHAT* DID MS. SOLINSKY JUST SAY?

"Excuse me," gasped an astonished, astounded, amazed, and goggle-eyed Lulu. "Did you just say 'spy'?"

"I did," Ms. Solinsky reluctantly replied. "I never should have said it—that was a terrible breach of security—but I did."

"You personally were trained to be a spy?" asked a stupefied Lulu.

"Trained and served as a spy," said Ms. Solinsky loudly and proudly—she was

clearly enjoying Lulu's adoring attention. "Code name Triple S."

(Another security breach—but never mind.)

CODE NAME? SHE HAD A CODE NAME? TRIPLE S WAS HER CODE NAME? LULU *LOVED IT*.

"So wait," Lulu said. "You trained and served as a spy and now you're . . ."

"A former spy. A retired spy. And, at present, a full-time babysitter whose specialty, you may recall, is babysitting especially difficult children."

The especially-difficult-children stuff should have made Lulu angry all over again. Except she was way too thrilled about the spy stuff.

She stood there, saying nothing, but

her brain was churning, churning. After which it churned and churned some more. After which came the following conversation:

Lulu: "A former spy. A retired spy. Not a spy anymore. But it sounds like you still remember how to do it."

Ms. Solinsky: "Of course I remember. Once a spy, always a spy."

Lulu: "And did you—may I call you Triple S?—did you, Triple S, have lots and lots of amazing spy adventures?"

Ms. Solinsky: "Amazing AND successful. In fact, I was so good at my work that I wound up being named Head of All Spy Training."

A spy so good that she was a trainer of spies! Lulu was so excited she hardly could breathe. She pressed a hand against her chest to calm her pounding heart and then asked the question that she was burning to ask.

"Would you, could you, please, dear Triple S"—did she just say *dear*?—"would you stay here and train me to be a spy?"

Train her to be a spy? Lulu wanted spy training from the very exact same woman about whom she'd repeatedly been chanting those most exceptionally unfriendly chants?

Ms. Solinsky looked long and coldly at Lulu. "Excuse me," she said, "but what's happened to all those cute little eeny meeny miney mos? What's happened to those photographs you were sending to your parents to get them to fly back home on the very next plane? Weren't you only recently trying all kinds of fiendish tricks to get me to go? And now, all of a sudden, you want me to *stay*?"

Lulu hung her head. She was actually
embarrassed. But Lulu being Lulu,
she only stayed embarrassed for a few
seconds.

"It's true," she told Ms. Solinsky, "that
I wanted you—the babysitter—to go. But
I definitely want you—the spy—to stay.
I just this minute decided that I want to
be a spy when I grow up. And you are the
perfect person to teach me how."

"Why would I want to do that?" asked
Ms. Solinsky.

"Because I really want you to," answered Lulu.

"That's IT?" said Ms. Solinsky. "Because you WANT me to? Do you usually get what you want just because you WANT it?"

"Usually," said Lulu. "Are you saying yes?"

"There's no reason in the world for me to say yes," said Ms. Solinsky.

"Actually, there is," said Lulu, a warning tone in her voice. "If I send out these

pictures of my wrecked room to my mom
and my dad, plus the entire universe,
everyone will think that you're the WORST
babysitter in town, maybe the world.
Sonia Sofia Solinsky, trained professional?
Hah! Your reputation would be . . . dog
poop!"

   "You are without a doubt," said Ms.
Solinsky, "the most especially difficult of
all the especially difficult children I've
babysat."

"But I wouldn't be," said Lulu, suddenly switching to a pretty-please tone of voice, "if I were being trained as a spy instead of being babysat by you. I'd obey your every command. I'd do whatever you told me to. I'd WANT to do brisk runs and bean-and-beet omelets. "

Ms. Solinsky, whose face had been as stern and as stony as something carved on a mountain, seemed to be softening—just a little bit. She did not want Lulu's parents to come home and

fire her. She did not want her reputation to be dog poop. And training a spy would certainly be more interesting than being a babysitter, even if the spy she'd be training was Lulu.

"TOTAL obedience?" she asked.

"Total," Lulu promised.

"I'll get back to you with my answer in an hour," said Ms. Solinsky. "Meanwhile, clean up as much of this mess as you can."

Lulu started to say no way was she

cleaning up this mess, and then she realized that wasn't a good idea. Instead, she stood up straight, clicked her heels, saluted, and said, "Yes, sir," to Ms. Solinsky. Except this time, she was saying it so earnestly, so respectfully, so politely that Ms. Solinsky wasn't not amused.

chapter fourteen

During the hour that Lulu
worked on her room and waited for Ms.
Solinsky's answer, she started chanting a
new, friendlier chant:

GFEDCBA,
Triple S has got to stay.
June or April, March or May,
Triple S has got to stay.

"She's GOT to stay and train me!" Lulu
kept saying to herself in between chants.
"I really really really really really want to
learn to be a spy."

Sixty minutes later, Ms. Solinsky, now toting her duffel bag, was standing once again in Lulu's bedroom. Looking around, she could see that though the room remained really wrecked, Lulu had tried hard to put it back together.

"I've considered your request," Ms. Solinsky told Lulu, "and I am prepared to offer a qualified yes. By 'qualified' I mean, first, you can't discuss the training with anybody. Ever. And second, if you challenge even one of my instructions, I will give up teaching you spy craft— at once!—and return—at once!—to babysitting you. Get it?"

Lulu was thrilled beyond thrilled. "I get it! Just give me my instructions. I want to learn *everything*!"

Today was still Sunday (in case you

forgot) and Lulu's parents were coming home Friday night, so Ms. Solinsky had only six days to train Lulu. And Lulu, of course, would also need time for her school and homework and trombone and dog-walking job, plus all her other busy, busy activities. But while Ms. Solinsky warned Lulu that becoming a full-fledged spy took *years* of training, "I'll have time to teach you a set of important basics."

Beginning, she announced, with Repair and Restore, which was also known as R and R.

Ms. Solinsky explained that spies, using special spy keys and other implements, can open any locked door they wish to open. However, she said, they may sometimes (like today) encounter certain obstacles (like a dresser) that require them to *crash* through a door instead. Spies also, said Ms. Solinsky, can leave any room that they have entered and searched (and wrecked) looking exactly as it had looked before, so that no one would ever know that they had been there. And that was why one of a spy's basic skills was Repair (fix whatever needs fixing) and Restore (make it look as if it never happened).

"And that," Ms. Solinsky told Lulu, "is what you now are going to do with your wrecked bedroom."

"Ridiculous! Impossible!" said Lulu, sounding like the old Lulu again.

"There's a great big hole in my door and my dresser drawers are all smashed up, and my trombone is dust, and my chair . . ."

"Do 'impossible' and 'ridiculous' mean you're refusing to obey?" Ms. Solinsky asked warningly.

"Of course that's what it . . . ," Lulu began, then—catching herself—continued, "DOESN'T mean. 'Impossible'? 'Ridiculous'? Not with Triple S as my spy teacher!"

"That is correct," Ms. Solinsky said, "and now"—she reached into her duffel bag—"let's get started."

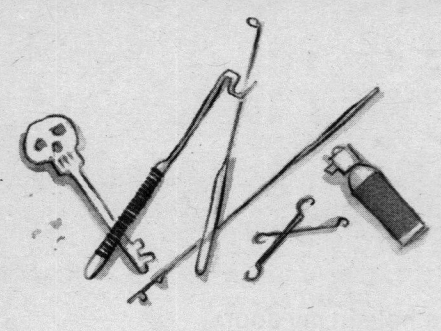

Out of her bag
came a jar of
extra-strength
rug wash, a large
tube of superglue, and a vacuum cleaner
designed to retrieve and reverse. (I'll
explain about that in just
a couple of seconds.)
Barking out instructions,
Ms. Solinsky guided
Lulu as she glued all the
broken pieces smoothly
together and scrubbed
that stinky green glop out of the rug,
then used the vacuum cleaner to suck up
(retrieve) all the trombone dust and rebuild
(reverse) that dust into a (believe it or
not!) as-good-as-new trombone.

When the work (most of which Lulu had
done) was finished, and the furniture
had been pushed back into place, no one
would ever have guessed that it had been

otherwise. No cracks where the breaks had been mended! No stain where the rug had been scrubbed! And when Lulu tested her rebuilt trombone, it (and she) sounded better than before!

"You have made a promising start," Ms. Solinsky told Lulu, who smiled a proud smile. "And now I need to see you destroy those pictures you took of the room in its wrecked condition. I can't take the slightest chance of having my reputation besmirched," which is a fancy way of saying "turned to dog poop."

Lulu kind of liked the idea of keeping those wrecked-room photographs in case she ran into problems with Ms. Solinsky. On the other hand she knew that there was only one thing she should do and that was . . . obey.

chapter fifteen

On Monday afternoon, after school, Lulu rushed into her house, yelling, "I'm home, Ms. Solinsky, and ready for training."

(Some clever readers will wonder why Ms. Solinsky wasn't waiting outside Lulu's school. Some even cleverer readers will figure out that it's because Ms. Solinsky is now Lulu's spy trainer— not her babysitter.)

There was no answer. Lulu yelled a few more times, then ran upstairs and checked out all the rooms, repeatedly calling Ms. Solinsky's name. Still no answer.

Back downstairs again, Lulu went racing from room to room, her heart beating fast as she called out, "Ms. Solinsky!" But the house was empty—at least it seemed empty—until Lulu reached the kitchen, where she saw someone sitting quietly on a chair. That someone definitely wasn't Ms. Solinsky.

What Lulu saw instead was a stranger—a woman as beautiful as a movie star—with long blond hair and big blue eyes and a slinky blue dress that perfectly matched

her eyes. And though, as we all know, our Lulu is not the kind of girl who frightens easily, she was shocked and alarmed to encounter this awesome blonde.

"*Who* are you?" Lulu demanded. "And *why* are you here? And *what* have you done with Ms. Sonia Sofia Solinsky?"

The beautiful stranger smiled at Lulu, tossed her long blond hair, and then replied in a voice as sweet as candy. "But, Lulu," she said to her, "I AM Ms. Solinsky."

Lulu was fainting. Well, not really fainting, but feeling so weak and wobbly in the knees that she had to sit herself down before she fell down. (And actually, though I'm the one writing this story, I also am feeling just a little faint.)

"I don't understand. I'm so confused." Lulu was almost babbling. "How can you be you when you have turned into a totally different person?"

Ms. Solinsky corrected her. "I have turned MYSELF into a different person. We're finished with R and R, and now we're moving on to basic spy lesson two, which is known as D and P—Disguise and Penetrate."

Ms. Solinsky explained that an extremely important spy-craft technique was the ability to Disguise your appearance so totally that even those closest to you wouldn't know you were you. Just as important, she added, was being able to Penetrate, see through, others' disguises, so you'd always be able to tell that they were them.

"We'll work on D and P today and tomorrow," Ms. Solinsky said to Lulu, who—completely recovered from her shock—said, "Great! Let's go!"

Ms. Solinsky explained that she had spent all Monday morning searching through her duffel bag for various items to transform Lulu into—

"Into who?" asked Lulu, exploding with curiosity. "Who will I be?"

"You'll see in due time," Ms. Solinsky said. "We'll do them one by one, and after each transformation you'll look in the mirror. But remember, I want no complaining and no argument."

No complaining? No argument? This was asking a lot—maybe too much—of Lulu.

Still, looking in the mirror after being disguised as a boy, Lulu had no complaints—she liked what she saw. With her hair tucked into a baseball cap, a sleek black leather jacket, and some fake brown freckles sprinkled across her nose, she'd been handsomely transformed from Lulu to Lou.

She was also okay—not thrilled, but okay—with the sight of herself disguised as a middle-aged woman, with glossy makeup, a raincoat, and high heels, though she certainly could have done without the ugly orange purse and the frizzy hair.

It was only when the mirror reflected—
to Lulu's absolute horror—a pudgy,
pigtailed three-year-old girl in pink
sneakers, pink ribbons, pink pants, and
a pink T-shirt that Lulu had to—she
desperately had to—say something.

(But before Lulu speaks, *I'd* like to say
that if these transformations seem kind
of impossible—and I'll be among the first
to admit that they do—it's because we do

not know the tricks of the trade. Spy craft can make anyone look shorter or taller; younger or older; female or male; animal, vegetable, or mineral. I may be writing this story, but the only folks here who know that stuff are Triple S, the former Head of All Spy Training, and Lulu, who is right now being trained.)

Except that maybe Lulu is about to stop being trained because—she cannot help herself—she simply HAS TO argue with Ms. Solinsky.

"A spy disguised as a pink and pigtailed

three-year-old? This is positively the dopiest, dumbest, stupidest thing I have ever heard in my life!"

Ms. Solinsky looked long and hard at Lulu. "And *this*," she said, "is gross insubordination"—a fancy way to say that you have seriously disobeyed me and you are doomed. "Since you have dared to question me, I hereby this minute resign as your spy trainer."

Lulu, in a panic, sunk to the floor and, actually begging on bended knees, asked Ms. Solinsky to give her one more chance.

And after a whole lot of "nos" from Ms. Solinsky and a whole lot of "please-please-please-please-pleases" from Lulu, Ms. Solinsky relented and said to Lulu, "I've already invested a great deal of time in your training. And therefore I will give you one more chance. I will also offer the following explanations, after which I will never again explain anything, and you never again will argue or complain."

Ms. Solinsky proceeded to explain:

"If you wanted to put a spy in a playground or preschool or day-care center, who's the LEAST suspicious person you could pick? The least suspicious person would be a little girl in pigtails, equipped with a hidden camera and a recording device. Have I made my point? Don't answer. Of course I have."

Ms. Solinsky cleared her throat again.

"And in order to prepare you for the next disguise we're doing, so you won't lose control when you look at yourself in the mirror, consider this question: If the bad guy you wanted to spy on was meeting another bad guy somewhere out in the country, with open fields and not a tree in sight, what disguise could you wear that would let you—without their having a clue—listen to every single word they said?"

Lulu, instead of trying to answer, took a look in the mirror. Calmly gazing back at her was . . . a cow.

chapter sixteen

$\mathcal{B}y$ the end of Monday, Lulu had learned to disguise herself as anyone and anything. She had also learned to notice all the little mistakes and carelessnesses that would tip her off when someone else was disguised. On Tuesday, Lulu's class would be taking a field trip to a museum, encountering many people during the day. Lulu's spy assignment was to figure out which of these people were actually an in-disguise Ms. Solinsky.

Early on Tuesday morning, an eager Lulu was up and dressed, confident that she would ace her assignment. But after she had startled the substitute teacher and the driver of the bus by whispering, "Gotcha. I know who you are!" when she didn't, she realized that she wasn't that great at Penetrate. Concentrating harder and using the spy craft that she had been taught, Lulu got better as the day went on, catching Ms. Solinsky disguised as a tour guide at the museum and a cashier at the cafeteria. Her greatest moment of triumph, however, came at the very end of the afternoon, when she shrewdly figured out that the dog that was sitting in front of her house when she got home from

school—a mutt that had peed profusely
on her sneakers—was actually none other
than Ms. Solinsky.

"I am impressed," Ms. Solinsky told
Lulu. "But don't get carried away with
yourself. We'll see, tomorrow, how well
you do when I'm teaching you H and C—
Hacking and Codes."

chapter seventeen

Hacking, Ms. Solinsky explained, was sneaking into other people's computers—computers sending out messages (like Lulu asking Mabel to bring over cats, or bad guys plotting how to destroy the world) that you definitely weren't ever supposed to read. Codes were ways of writing your top-secret messages so secretly that, even when hackers read what you had written, they couldn't understand a single word.

Working with Lulu on Wednesday, Ms. Solinsky first taught her several nifty codes and then moved on to the tricks of hacking computers, solemnly explaining to her, "Hacking is wrong and not nice and against the law, but you need to learn how to do it to be a good spy."

"And I do want to be a good spy. I do!" said Lulu—and then she dug in and learned how to hack faster than she had learned anything else in her life.

"You've got a natural talent," Ms. Solinsky said to Lulu. "But don't use it except when you're an official spy. Because if you're hacking to find out if Henry likes you better than he likes Nora Kaplan, you probably won't appreciate the answer."

"I have no idea what you're talking about," Lulu told Ms. Solinsky, who patted her on her shoulder and replied, "You are *so* much better at hacking than at lying."

chapter eighteen

GFEDCBA,
Triple S has got to stay.
June or April, March or May,
Triple S has got to stay.
Oink or quack or moo or neigh,
Triple S has got to stay.
Austin, Boston, Santa Fe,
Triple S has got to stay.

Lulu was chanting her friendly new chant as she fell asleep that night, wondering what Ms. Solinsky would teach her next. After Repair and Restore, Disguise and Penetrate, Hacking and Codes, she hardly could wait for the lesson that Thursday would bring.

chapter nineteen

Back from school on Thursday, Lulu was met at the door by Sonia Sofia Solinsky, who said to her, "We must hurry. Your parents return tomorrow night. Which means we haven't much time for me to give you your final lesson in basic spy craft."

She explained that this final lesson involved several clues that she had hidden all over the house, with each clue leading onward to the next. If Lulu succeeded in following them—which wouldn't be easy to do—she would find, at the end, what the clues had been leading her to.

"Which is what?" Lulu asked. "Tell me, and I'll get started. I'll get started right now and be finished before bedtime."

"I wouldn't count on being done before bedtime," said Ms. Solinsky. "And you aren't permitted to know in advance what you'll find. In fact, this particular lesson, which ends each set of my spy-craft lessons, is known as"—HERE IT COMES, FOLKS! HERE IT COMES!—"MM, which stands for"—YES!—"Mysterious Mission."

(And *that*, I sincerely hope, takes care of *that*!)

MYSTERIOUS MISSION! Lulu totally loved it. And she knew without a doubt that she would succeed. Indeed, by now she was positive that she was the best spy-in-training that Sonia Sofia Solinsky—code name Triple S—had ever trained.

"Aren't I the best spy-in-training that you have ever trained?" Lulu asked Ms. Solinsky.

"Let's not get pushy," Ms. Solinsky replied. Then she sat Lulu down in the kitchen, fed her an early supper, and handed her—printed neatly on a note card—the clue to where she should look for her next clue:

They have their ups.
They have their downs.
You do not like to use them.
This is the seventh one you've owned.
Because you always lose them.
Look inside it.
That's where I decided

To hide it.

Lulu narrowed her eyes as she read and re-read and then re-re-read the clue. She read it to herself, and she read it out loud. After which she turned to Ms. Solinsky and asked, in a quite snippy tone of voice, "What kind of dopey, dumb, stupid clue is *that*?"

Good grief—has Lulu forgotten total obedience?

"Excuse me," said Ms. Solinsky. "What did you say?"

Lulu, pulling herself together in the nick of time, replied, "Oh, I only just was saying

that this clue is kind of confusing and was
wondering if you could give me a little
help."

"Careful attention to each of the
words," Ms. Solinsky replied, "ought to
give you all the help you need. And now
I'm going up to my room and I don't wish
to be disturbed. You're on your own."

At the top of the stairs, however, Ms.
Solinsky stopped for a moment. "Inside
it. Decided. Hide it," she said. "As you can
see, my little spy-in-training, you're not
the only one who knows how to rhyme."

You clever folks reading this story have
doubtlessly already figured out what this
clue was referring to. But it took Lulu
quite a while to think of what goes up and
down, and how she complains whenever
her mom makes her use one, and that
she had already lost a green one, a blue

one, a plaid one, two flowered ones, and
a frog one, making the yellow polka-dot
one that hung in the front-hall closet her
seventh . . . UMBRELLA.

Lulu rushed to that closet, reached
inside the hanging umbrella, and found
her next clue:

In something that rhymes with FOX
Is something that rhymes with EYES,
And taped to that second something
   is a clue.
You'll discover it all by yourself
On something that rhymes with ELF,
And there's even something for
   breakfast tomorrow too.

Two hours later, and getting close to her bedtime, Lulu came up—at last!—with BOX and PRIZE and SHELF and BREAKFAST CEREAL. Rummaging through the cereal *boxes* that stood on a *shelf* in the kitchen, she eventually pulled out of the Toasted Yummy Extra-Sugar Bits a purple plastic superhero—the *prize*—on the back of which was scotch-taped her next clue:

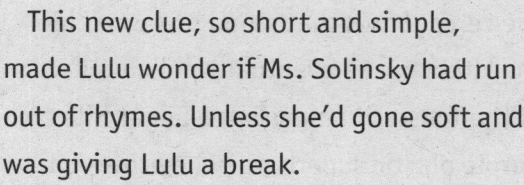

Inside of a shoe,
  near the toe,
Awaits what you
  next need to know.

This new clue, so short and simple,
made Lulu wonder if Ms. Solinsky had run
out of rhymes. Unless she'd gone soft and
was giving Lulu a break.

But three hours later, and way way past
her bedtime, Lulu had found no clue in
the toe of a shoe, though she'd gone
through every shoe in her closet, as well
as every shoe of her mom's and her
dad's, and had even checked out
Ms. Solinsky's combat
boots. Disgusted,
discouraged, and

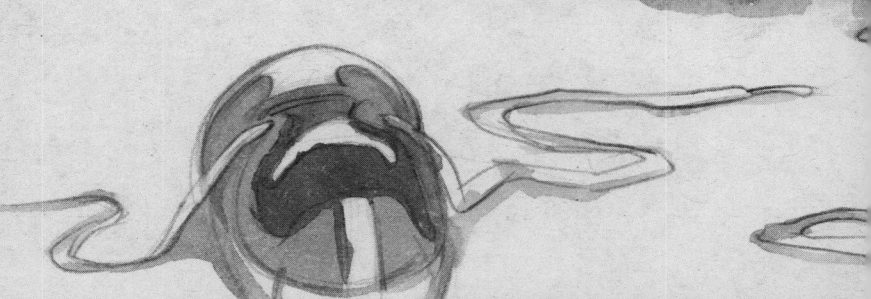

exhausted, she lay down on her
bed to rest for a few minutes and
discovered—when she slipped off her
sneakers—guess what?

That's right! She found a note card,
neatly tucked into her left sneaker,
near her big toe. And what we'd all
like to know (and that includes me) is
how, and also when, did that clue get
in there?

chapter twenty

Lulu couldn't wait to read the next clue, which went like this:

Open the striped curtain.
Raise the wooden blind.
Close the window all the way
And maybe you will find
What you are looking for.

There was only one room in the house with a striped curtain and wooden blind, and that was the bathroom next to Lulu's bedroom. And sure enough, when she opened and raised and closed, as she'd been instructed, there was a note card taped onto the window. Unfortunately, the note card said:

YES, MAYBE YOU WILL FIND IT.
AND MAYBE YOU WON'T.

Under that message, in smaller print, was
another message:

So what do you think?
Is it under the sink?

Lulu looked under the bathroom sink, where
she found another message:

NO, IT ISN'T!

Obviously, Ms. Solinsky was messing with
her. Speaking out loud in the empty room, a
disgusted Lulu announced, "I am not amused."
Below that message, however, was
what seemed like a serious clue, a clue that
Lulu was finding hard to read. She was finding
it hard to read and even harder to understand

because her eyes kept closing with
exhaustion. It said:

> In the living room, cleverly hidden,
> Is the very last clue I have written,
> Leading you directly to your goal.
> You must rhyme what you need to
>   find first
> With the opposite of WORST,
> On top of which is a thing that rhymes
>   with HOLE.
> And that thing that is rhyming with
>   HOLE,
> (As well as with POLE and with ROLL)
> Is filled with things you can reach your
>   hand in and take.
> But although all these things rhyme
>   with CUTE

(And BOOT, SUIT, TOOT, and LOOT)
The one that you are looking for is
   a fake.

   Lulu didn't think much of a poem
that had the utter nerve to rhyme
"written" and "hidden," but by now she
was so sleepy that she couldn't think
about anything but sleep. "I need to
go to bed. I have to get some sleep. I'll
get some sleep, and I'll wake up real

early tomorrow, and before I even eat
breakfast, I'll figure this out."

Early on Friday morning, however,
nothing got figured out. Lulu was still
too sleepy and too fuzzy-headed. Besides
which, this clue was really really HARD!
(Maybe some of you DON'T think it's hard,
in which case, smarty pantses, step right
up and give us the answer right now. As
for the rest of you—feel free to read on.)

Anyway, it was not until late in the
morning—while Lulu was learning state
capitals in her geography class—that
CHEST (which rhymes with BEST, which is

the opposite of WORST) and BOWL (which rhymes with HOLE and POLE and ROLL) all of a sudden popped into her brain, along with FRUIT (which rhymes with CUTE, plus BOOT, SUIT, TOOT, and LOOT). Then she had to wait for over four more maddening hours until—at last!—school was over and she could go home. And reach her hand down till she found—among the real FRUIT in the BOWL on the living room CHEST—an apple that was definitely fake. And read the clue that was hidden inside the fake apple. And follow that final clue to what she was looking for. It said:

Search no more. Search no more.
It's inside the chest, in the bottom
   drawer.

And it was!

chapter twenty-one

While Lulu was busy searching, Ms. Solinsky watched and waited, not saying a single word till Lulu plucked, from that bottom drawer, a silver disk that hung from a silver chain and upon which were boldly inscribed the letters MM. Then, standing at her tallest and straightest, Ms. Solinsky declared, "Mission accomplished." After which she carefully clasped the chain—with its gleaming disk—around Lulu's neck.

"This disk," she said, "hereby certifies that you have completed your first Mysterious Mission. My hearty congratulations, Double L."

Lulu was almost fainting, this time with joy. "You're giving me a code name? I've got my very own code name? From now on everyone calls me Double L?"

"I'm afraid I must remind you," Ms. Solinsky coldly replied, "that this is what's known as a covert operation. And covert means secret, undercover, hush-hush. You may not tell anyone—ANYONE; unless they're a fellow spy—your code name or that you're being trained in spy craft. And you'll need to remove that disk from your neck before anybody sees it, and put it away where nobody ever will."

But Lulu was now in her most impossible, give-me-what-I-want mode. Meaning that she was being a pain in the butt. "I hate this! I hate this a lot! I really hate this!" she said. "I want to wear my silver disk. I want to be called Double L. What's the point of being a spy if I can't tell Mabel and Fleischman,

and all the kids at school, and Harry
Potter"—she meant the other Harry
Potter—"and my mom and my dad and Mr.
B and . . . everyone?"

Ms. Solinsky began unclasping Lulu's
silver chain. "We'll do it my way, or I take
back your disk. Furthermore, I'll deny
whatever you say about me, or you, being
a spy. I'll swear that you're making it
up, that you're telling lies, that you're
imagining things. And I'll say it so many
times that very soon your reputation will
be . . . dog poop."

Ms. Solinsky looked at her watch. "Your
parents," she said, "will be here in a
couple of hours. You'd better decide what
you are going to do."

There was a heavy silence in the living
room. Lulu silently stared at Ms. Solinsky.

Ms. Solinsky silently stared back. Ten, fifteen, twenty, twenty-five minutes went by before they even started talking. And it wasn't until a few seconds before Lulu's mom and her dad were due home, that Lulu and Ms. Solinsky cut a deal.

Lulu, much as she hated it, swore never to mention her spy training or her code name, and promised to hide her disk in a safe place. Ms. Solinsky swore to train Lulu in spy craft whenever Lulu's mom and her dad went away. She also solemnly promised that when Lulu grew up and applied for a job as a spy, she'd write a letter saying nice things about her. Unless Lulu didn't deserve having nice things said about her. Or unless Lulu changed her mind and decided she'd rather be president of the United States.

But then Lulu's parents came home and almost ruined everything!

Rushing through the door and dropping their suitcases on the floor, they threw their arms around Lulu and started sobbing.

"Oh, my precious! My darling! My treasure!" wailed her weeping mom. "We missed you so very much! We hardly could stand it!"

"Oh, pumpkin. Oh, sweet pea!" her dad said, hugging her tight and soaking her shoulder with his hot tears. "It was awful being without you. We will never, never, ever do this again!"

Lulu was instantly on alert. "Do what again?" she demanded.

Her parents answered together. "We will never go away without you. Never!"

Lulu was shocked beyond shocked. This was a nightmare! A disaster! A catastrophe! She felt that she was about to lose her mind! How would Ms. Solinsky be able to train her to be a spy if her parents were never going to leave her behind?

"You HAVE to, you've GOT to, you NEED

to take more vacations!" Lulu shouted.
"You need some private, grown-ups-only
time. You've got to go away a lot, and I will
be just fine being babysat by DARLING Ms.
Solinsky."

Lulu was now jumping up and down—and
although it wasn't a tantrum, it was close—
shouting, "Go! You have to go! Go! Go! Go!"

Lulu's mom and her dad were dazed and
perplexed and completely confused and
full of questions: What was going on here?
What was she saying? Why was she acting in
this peculiar way? Hadn't she, only a week

ago, carried on most unpleasantly when they told her that they were going away without her? So why was she now insisting that she WANTED them to go away without her?

"Lulu, sweetie . . . ," her mom began.

"Lulu, honey . . . ," her dad began.

"What's gotten into you?" they asked together.

And Lulu, looking first at her mom and then at her dad, replied, "I guess I'm just an extremely difficult child."

chapter twenty-two

You won't be surprised to hear that after at least an hour of quite intense discussion, Lulu—as she so often did—got her way. This meant persuading her mom and her dad (though they swore they would miss her to pieces) to go off on lots of trips and vacations without her.

It also meant making them promise that whenever they left town, they'd put her in the care of Ms. Solinsky. Who, to their bewilderment, seemed to have won their daughter's undying affection. And who, looking great in stiletto heels, loose hair, and a slinky blue dress (she only wore the uniform to intimidate extremely difficult kids) was saying good-bye to everyone and rushing off for a date with Harry Potter.

• • •

And so, from that time on, Triple S came
to stay—several times a year—with Double
L, giving her lessons in spy craft, except
when she needed to be disciplined for
too much arguing and too little obeying.
For Lulu, you won't be surprised to
hear, continued to be difficult, though
not as extremely as she used to be. And
whenever she was, she was handed a little
toothbrush and a bucket of soapy water
and told to scrub the steps in front of her
house.

What made Lulu keep being difficult
was her absolute conviction that she
was the greatest spy-in-training ever.
And though, no doubt about it, she was
truly gifted and talented, she constantly
got into trouble because she constantly
wanted to do too much too soon.

Like trying to wreck, then Restore and
Repair, that tree by her bathroom window.

(Except that because Lulu's wrecking was so much better than her restoring, it required all of Ms. Solinsky's spy-craft skills to rescue the poor tree.)

Or like trying to Disguise herself as a helicopter. (It took Ms. Solinsky less than two seconds to Penetrate Lulu's disguise because most helicopters do not wear knee socks.)

Or like trying to Hack—imagine! The nerve!—into Ms. Solinsky's computer. (Except that when she did, she found that every single item of information—including some personal e-mails from Harry Potter—had been transcribed into an unbreakable Code.)

Or like trying to create a Mysterious Mission, complete with clues, for Ms. Solinsky to figure out and follow. (But

Ms. Solinsky figured them out almost as
fast as she read them, except when she
almost choked on the clue that Lulu had
cut up into little pieces and mixed into her
morning bean-and-beet omelet.)

After the b-and-b incident, Ms. Solinsky
spoke a few words to Lulu. She spoke in
a slow and soft and most serious voice.
"You may be pretty good, Double L,"
she told her. "But you aren't—repeat,
AREN'T—good enough yet!"

Lulu hung her head and tried to look
sincerely embarrassed. But—let's be
honest here—she wasn't embarrassed. In

fact, she was feeling extremely proud of
the stuff she had tried to do, even though
it hadn't exactly worked out. In fact,
she was feeling quite positive that even
though she might not be good enough
YET, she surely would be much more than
good enough SOON.

However, she continued—in the interest
of not making trouble—to hang her head.

Ms. Solinsky, who knew very well how to
tell a truly embarrassed girl from a fake
one, gave Lulu an oh-so-understanding
smile.

After which she presented her, as
she would for years to come, with a
toothbrush and a bucket of soapy water.

The

End